IT IS NIGHT

by PHYLLIS ROWAND

pictures by LAURA DRONZEK

Greenwillow Books

An Imprint of HarperCollins Publishers

Acrylic paints were used to prepare the full-color art.
The text type is 24-point Contax.

Library of Congress Cataloging-in-Publication Data

Rowand, Phyllis, (date)
It is night / by Phyllis Rowand ; illustrated by Laura Dronzek
pages cm
"Greenwillow Books."
Originally published in 1953 by Harper & Row, with illustrations by
the author.
Summary: "A little girl says good night to a seal, a bear, a lion,
a train, and so on—giving readers a bit of information about
each"—Provided by publisher.
ISBN 978-0-06-225024-7 (trade ed.)
[1. Bedtime—Fiction. 2. Animals—Fiction. 3. Toys—Fiction.]
I. Dronzek, Laura, illustrator. II. Title.
PZ7.R79It 2014 [E]—dc23 2013028060

14 15 16 17 18 SCP 10 9 8 7 6 5 4 3 2 1
First Edition

Greenwillow Books

For Fogerty, Adnap, Nana, Petit, Sunday, Pink, Richard, Mrs. Ippi, The thump,
Padula, Old dear, the seven bears, and all those others who live upstairs—P. R.

For Will and Clara—L. D.

It is night.

Where should a big brown bear sleep?

When it is cold, in a cozy cave.

And when it is warm, a bed of leaves

under the sweet-smelling pine is fine for him.

Where would a rooster roost?

In a chicken coop.

A rabbit, of course, if he has his own way,
will go hopping at night and sleep all the day. . . .
Where would be a good bed for a rabbit?

In a cabbage.

Except that he would want to eat it.

And he couldn't sleep in it and eat it too.

Where should a duck settle down for the night?

In the tall grass at the water's edge,
with his head tucked under his wing.

Where does a little cat curl up at night?

Her own special basket is what she would like,
with a lining of wooly warmth or smooth silk.

Where should a seal rest his sleek head?

On the quiet beach of a faraway island,
or safe in an island cave.

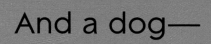

And a dog—

belongs outdoors in a doghouse.
So he can keep an eye on the stars
and see that they don't bump into the moon.

Where would be a good big bed
for a good big elephant?

A place deep in the dark jungle,
under the heavy forest trees.
A tiger, a lion, a zebra, a giraffe would like that too.

Where does a railroad train go at night?

If it is going somewhere, it goes there.
And if it is not, it stands still on the tracks.

And dolls—big and small—
where do they belong at the end of the happy day?

Tucked away in their own big and little beds
after the long hours of play.

Where does a mouse sleep?

If he is a house mouse, somewhere in a house. And if he is a field mouse, the tall grasses keep his tiny self safe.

And a monkey?

He should be hiding high in a tree—
his tail twisting round and around—
to keep him from falling down,
down to the ground.

These would be good beds for all of these.
But do they sleep there?

They sleep in the bed of one small child . . .

ALL OF THEM.

The bear, the lion, the large and small dolls,
the elephant. The zebra, the mouse, the rooster,
the dog, the cat. The giraffe, the duck, the seal,
the railroad train, the tiger.

They all crowd into that one bed every night.
But the child doesn't care.
The child loves them all, and wants them there.
This is the bed for that small child.

Sweet sleep, small one—
snug in your own big world.
Safe in your own little bed, sleep tight.

It is night.